# LARGE PRINT BOOKS FICTION: AGATHA CHRISTIE SHORT MYSTERY STORIES

## ILLUSTRATED COLLECTION

Agatha Christie

Lambda Press

# Contents

# Chapter 1

# The Wife of the Kenite

Herr Schaefer removed his hat and wiped his perspiring brow. He was hot. He was hungry and thirsty—especially the latter. But, above all, he was anxious. Before him stretched the yellow expanse of the veldt. Behind him, the line of the horizon was broken by the 'dumps' of the outlying portion of the Reef. And from far away, in the direction of Johannesburg, came a sound like distant thunder. But it was not thunder, as Herr Schaefer knew only too well. It was monotonous and regular, and represented the triumph of law and order over the forces of Revolution.

Herr Schaefer

Incidentally, it was having a most wearing effect on the nerves of Herr Schaefer. The position in which he found himself was an unpleasant one. The swift efficient proclamation of martial law, followed by the dramatic arrival of Smuts with the tyres of his car shot flat, had had the effect of completely disorganising the carefully laid plans of Schaefer and his friends, and Schaefer himself had narrowly escaped being laid by the heels. For the moment he was at large, but the present was uncomfortable, and the future too problematical to be pleasant.

In good, sound German, Herr Schaefer cursed the country, the climate, the Rand and all workers thereon, and most especially his late employers, the Reds.

As a paid agitator, he had done his work with true German efficiency, but his military upbringing, and his years of service with the German Army in Belgium, led him to admire the forcefulness of Smuts, and to despise unfeignedly the untrained rabble, devoid of discipline, which had crumbled to pieces at the first real test.

'They are scum,' said Herr Schaefer, gloomily, moistening his cracked lips. 'Swine! No drilling. No order. No discipline. Ragged commandos riding loose about the veldt! Ah! If they had but one Prussian drill sergeant!'

Involuntarily his back straightened. For a year he had been endeavouring to cultivate a slouch which, together with a ragged beard, might make his apparent dealing in such innocent vegetable produce as cabbages, cauliflowers, and potatoes less open to doubt. A momentary shiver went down his spine as he reflected that certain papers might even now be in the hands of the military—papers whereon the word 'cabbage' stood opposite 'dynamite', and potatoes were labelled 'detonators'.

The sun was nearing the horizon. Soon the cool of the evening would set in. If he could only reach a friendly farm (there were one or two hereabouts, he knew), he would find shelter for the night, and explicit directions that might set him on the road to freedom on the morrow.

Suddenly his eyes narrowed appreciatively upon a point to his extreme left.

'Mealies!' said Herr Schaefer. 'Where there are mealies there is a farm not far off.'

His reasoning proved correct. A rough track led through the cultivated belt of land. He came first to a cluster of kraals, avoided them dextrously (since he had no wish to be seen if the farm should not prove to be one of those he sought), and skirting a slight rise, came suddenly upon the farm itself. It was the usual low building, with a corrugated roof, and a stoep running round two sides of it.

The sun was setting now, a red, angry blur on the horizon, and a woman was standing in the open doorway, looking out into the falling dusk. Herr Schaefer pulled his hat well over his eyes and came up the steps.

'Is this by any chance the farm of Mr Henshel?' he asked.

The woman nodded without speaking, staring at him with wide blue eyes.

Schaefer drew a deep breath of relief, and looked back at her with a measure of appreciation. He admired the Dutch, wide-bosomed type such as this. A grand creature, with her full breast and her wide hips; not young, nearer forty than thirty, fair hair just touched with grey parted simply in the middle of her wide forehead, something grand and forceful about her, like a patriarch's wife of old.

'A fine mother of sons,' thought Herr Schaefer appreciatively. 'Also, let us hope, a good cook!'

His requirements of women were primitive and simple.

'Mr Henshel expects me, I think,' said the German, and added in a slightly lower tone: 'I am interested in potatoes.'

She gave the expected reply.

'We, too, are cultivators of vegetables.' She spoke the words correctly, but with a strong accent. Her English was evidently not her strong point and Schaefer put her down as belonging to one of those Dutch Nationalist families who forbid their children to use the interloper's tongue. With a big, work-stained hand, she pointed behind him.

'You come from Jo'burg—yes?'

He nodded.

'Things are finished there. I escaped by the skin of my teeth. Then I lost myself on the veldt. It is pure chance that I found my way here.'

The Dutch woman shook her head. A strange ecstatic smile irradiated her broad features.

'There is no chance—only God. Enter, then.'

Approving her sentiments, for Herr Schaefer liked a woman to be religious, he crossed the threshold. She drew back to let him pass, the smile still lingering on her face, and just for a moment the thought that there was something here he did not quite understand flashed across Herr Schaefer's mind. He dismissed the idea as of little importance.

The house was built, like most, in the form of an H. The inner hall, from which rooms opened out all round, was pleasantly cool. The table was spread in preparation for a meal. The woman showed him to a bedroom, and on his return to the hall, when he had removed the boots from his aching feet, he found Henshel awaiting him. An Englishman, this, with a mean, vacuous face, a little rat of a fellow drunk with catchwords and phrases. It was amongst such as he that most of Schaefer's work had lain, and he knew the type well. Abuse of capitalists, of the 'rich who batten on the poor', the iniquities of the Chamber of Mines, the heroic endurance of the miners—these were the topics on which Henshel expatiated, Schaefer nodding wearily with his mind fixed solely on food and drink.

At last the woman appeared, bearing a steaming tureen of soup. They sat down together and fell to. It was good soup.

Henshel continued to talk; his wife was silent. Schaefer contented himself with monosyllables and appropriate grunts. When Mrs Henshel left the room to bring in the next course, he said appreciatively: 'Your wife is a good cook. You are lucky. Not all Dutch women cook well.'

Henshel stared at him.

'My wife is not Dutch.'

Schaefer looked his astonishment, but the shortness of Henshel's tone, and some unacknowledged uneasiness in himself forbade him asking further. It was odd, though. He had been so sure that she was Dutch.

After the meal, he sat on the stoep in the cool dusk smoking. Somewhere in the house behind him a door banged. It was followed by the noise of a horse's hoofs. Vaguely uneasy, he sat forward listening as they grew fainter in the distance, then started violently to find Mrs Henshel standing at his elbow with a steaming cup of coffee. She set it down on a little table beside him.

'My husband has ridden over to Cloete's—to make the arrangements for getting you away in the morning,' she explained.

'Oh! I see.'

Curious, how his uneasiness persisted.

'When will he be back?'

'Some time after midnight.'

His uneasiness was not allayed. Yet what was it that he feared? Surely not that Henshel would give him up to the police? No, the man was sincere enough—a red-hot Revolutionist. The fact of the matter was that he, Conrad Schaefer, had got nerves! A German soldier (Schaefer unconsciously always thought of himself as a soldier) had no business with nerves. He took up the cup beside him and drank it down, making a grimace as he did so. What filthy stuff this Boer coffee always was! Roasted acorns! He was sure of it—roasted acorns!

He put the cup down again, and as he did so, a deep sigh came from the woman standing by his side. He had almost forgotten her presence.

'Will you not sit down?' he asked, making no motion, however, to rise from his own seat.

She shook her head.

'I have to clear away, and wash the dishes, and make my house straight.'

Schaefer nodded an approving head.

'The children are already in bed, I suppose,' he said genially.

There was a pause before she answered.

'I have no children.'

Schaefer was surprised. From the first moment he saw her he had definitely associated her with motherhood.

She took up the cup and walked to the entrance door with it. Then she spoke over her shoulder.

'I had one child. It died . . .'

'Ach! I am sorry,' said Schaefer, kindly.

The woman did not answer. She stood there motionless. And suddenly Schaefer's uneasiness returned a hundred-fold. Only this time, he connected it definitely—not with the house, not with Henshel, but with this slow-moving, grandly fashioned woman—this wife of Henshel's who was neither English nor Dutch. His curiosity roused afresh, he asked her the question point blank. What nationality was she?

'Flemish.'

She said the word abruptly, then passed into the house, leaving Herr Schaefer disturbed and upset.

Flemish! That was it, was it? Flemish! His mind flew swiftly to and fro, from the mud flats of Belgium to the sun-baked plateaus of South Africa. Flemish! He didn't like it. Both the French and the Belgians were so extraordinarily unreasonable! They couldn't forget.

His mind felt curiously confused. He yawned two or three times, wide, gaping yawns. He must get to bed and sleep—sleep—. Pah! How bitter that coffee had been—he could taste it still.

A light sprang up in the house. He got up and made his way to the door. His legs felt curiously unsteady. Inside, the big woman was sitting reading by the light of a small oil lamp. Herr Schaefer felt strangely reassured at the sight of the heavy volume on her knee. The Bible! He approved of women reading the Bible. He was a religious man himself, with a thorough belief in the German God, the God of the Old Testament, a God of blood and battles, of thunder and lightning, of material rewards and dire material vengeance, swift to anger and terrible in wrath.

He stumbled to a chair (what was the matter with his legs?); and in a thick, strange voice, suppressing another terrific yawn, he asked her what chapter she was reading.

Her blue eyes, under their level brows met his, something inscrutable in their

depths. So might have looked a prophet-
ess of Israel.

'The fourth chapter of Judges.'

He nodded, yawning again. He must go
to bed . . . but the effort to rise was too
much for him . . . his eyelids closed . . .

'The fourth chapter of Judges.' What was
the fourth chapter of Judges? His uneasiness returned, swelled into terror.
Something was wrong . . . Judges . . .
Sleep overcame him. He went down into
the depths—and horror went with him .
. .

He awoke, dragging himself back to consciousness . . . Time had passed—much time, he felt certain of it. Where was he? He blinked up at the light—there were pains in his arms and legs . . . he felt sick . . . the taste of the coffee was still in his mouth . . . But what was this? He was lying on the floor, bound hand and foot with strips of towel, and standing over him was the sinister figure of the woman who was not Dutch. His wits came back to him in a flash of sheer desperate fear. He was in danger . . . great danger . . .

...standing over him was the sinister figure of the woman

She marked the growth of conscious-ness in his eyes, and answered it as though he had actually spoken.

'Yes, I will tell you now. You remember passing through a place called Voog-plaat, in Belgium?'

He recalled the name. Some twopen-ny-ha'penny village he had passed through with his regiment.

She nodded, and went on.

'You came to my door with some other soldiers. My man was away with the Belgian Army. My first man—not Henshel, I have only been married to him two years. The boy, my little one—he was only four years of age—ran out. He began to cry—what child would not? He feared the soldiers. You ordered him to stop. He could not. You seized a chopper—ah God!—and struck off his hand! You laughed, and said: "That hand will never wield a weapon against Germany."'

'It is not true,' cried Schaefer, shrilly, 'And even if it was—it was war!'

She paid no heed, but went on.

'I struck you in the face. What mother would not have done otherwise? You caught up the child . . . and dashed him against the wall . . .'

She stopped, her voice broken, her breast heaving . . .

Schaefer murmured feebly, abandoning the idea of denial.

'It was war . . . it was war . . .'

The sweat stood on his brow. He was alone with this woman, miles from help . . .

'I recognised you at once this afternoon in spite of your beard. You did not recognise me. You said it was chance led you here—but I knew it was God . . .'

Her bosom heaved, her eyes flashed with a fanatical light. Her God was Schaefer's God—a God of vengeance. She was uplifted by the strange, stern frenzy of a Priestess of old.

'He has delivered you into my hands.'

Wild words poured from Schaefer, arguments, prayers, appeals for mercy, threats. And all left her untouched.

'God sent me another sign. When I opened the Bible tonight, I saw what He would have me do. Blessed above women shall Jael, the wife of Heber the Kenite, be . . .'

She stooped and took from the floor a hammer and some long, shining nails . . . A scream burst from Schaefer's throat. He remembered now the fourth chapter of Judges, that dramatic story of black inhospitality! Sisera fleeing from his enemies . . . a woman standing at the door of a tent . . . Jael, the wife of Heber the Kenite . . .

And sonorously, in her deep voice with the broad Flemish accent, her eyes shining as the Israelite woman's may have shone in bygone days, she spoke the words of triumph:

'This is the day in which the Lord hath delivered mine enemy into my hand . . .'

# Chapter 2

# The Affair At The Victory Ball

I

Hercule Poirot

Pure chance led my friend Hercule Poirot, formerly chief of the Belgian force, to be connected with the Styles Case. His success brought him notoriety, and he decided to devote himself to the solving of problems in crime. Having been wounded on the Somme and invalided out of the Army, I finally took up my quarters with him in London. Since I have a firsthand knowledge of most of his cases, it has been suggested to me that I select some of the most interesting and place them on record. In doing so, I feel that I cannot do better than begin with that strange tangle which aroused such widespread public interest at the time. I refer to the affair at the Victory Ball.

Although perhaps it is not so fully demonstrative of Poirot's peculiar methods as some of the more obscure cases, its sensational features, the well-known people involved, and the tremendous publicity given it by the press, make it stand out as a cause célèbre and I have long felt that it is only fitting that Poirot's connection with the solution should be given to the world.

It was a fine morning in spring, and we were sitting in Poirot's rooms. My little friend, neat and dapper as ever, his egg-shaped head tilted on one side, was delicately applying a new pomade to his moustache. A certain harmless vanity was a characteristic of Poirot's and fell into line with his general love of order and method. The Daily Newsmonger, which I had been reading, had slipped to the floor, and I was deep in a brown study when Poirot's voice recalled me.

"Of what are you thinking so deeply, mon ami?"

"To tell you the truth," I replied, "I was puzzling over this unaccountable affair at the Victory Ball. The papers are full of it." I tapped the sheet with my finger as I spoke.

"Yes?"

"The more one reads of it, the more shrouded in mystery the whole thing becomes!" I warmed to my subject. "Who killed Lord Cronshaw? Was Coco Courtenay's death on the same night a mere coincidence? Was it an accident? Or did she deliberately take an overdose of cocaine?" I stopped, and then added dramatically: "These are the questions I ask myself."

Poirot, somewhat to my annoyance, did not play up. He was peering into the glass, and merely murmured: "Decidedly, this new pomade, it is a marvel for the moustaches!" Catching my eye, however, he added hastily: "Quite so—and how do you reply to your questions?"

But before I could answer, the door opened, and our landlady announced Inspector Japp. The Scotland Yard man was an old friend of ours and we greeted him warmly.

"Ah, my good Japp," cried Poirot, "and what brings you to see us?"

"Well, Monsieur Poirot," said Japp, seating himself and nodding to me, "I'm on a case that strikes me as being very much in your line, and I came along to know whether you'd care to have a finger in the pie?"

Poirot had a good opinion of Japp's abilities, though deploring his lamentable lack of method, but I, for my part, considered that the detective's highest talent lay in the gentle art of seeking favours under the guise of conferring them!

"It's the Victory Ball," said Japp persuasively. "Come, now, you'd like to have a hand in that."

Poirot smiled at me.

"My friend Hastings would, at all events. He was just holding forth on the subject, n'est-ce pas, mon ami?"

"Well, sir," said Japp condescendingly, "you shall be in it too. I can tell you, it's something of a feather in your cap to have inside knowledge of a case like this. Well, here's to business. You know the main facts of the case, I suppose, Monsieur Poirot?"

"From the papers only—and the imagination of the journalist is sometimes misleading.

Recount the whole story to me."

Japp crossed his legs comfortably and began.

Inspector Japp

"As all the world and his wife knows, on Tuesday last a grand Victory Ball was held. Every twopenny-halfpenny hop calls itself that nowadays, but this was the real thing, held at the Colossus Hall, and all London at it—including your Lord Cronshaw and his party."

"His dossier?" interrupted Poirot. "I should say his bioscope—no, how do you call it— biograph?"

"Viscount Cronshaw was fifth viscount, twenty-five years of age, rich, unmarried, and very fond of the theatrical world. There were rumours of his being engaged to Miss Courtenay of the Albany Theatre, who was known to her friends as 'Coco' and who was, by all accounts, a very fascinating young lady."

"Good. Continuez!"

"Lord Cronshaw's party consisted of six people: he himself, his uncle, the Honourable Eustace Beltane, a pretty American widow, Mrs. Mallaby, a young actor, Chris Davidson, his wife, and last but not least, Miss Coco Courtenay. It was a fancy dress ball, as you know, and the Cronshaw party represented the old Italian Comedy—whatever that may be."

"The Commedia dell' Arte," murmured Poirot. "I know."

"Anyway, the costumes were copied from a set of china figures forming part of Eustace Beltane's collection. Lord Cronshaw was Harlequin; Beltane was Punchinello; Mrs. Mallaby matched him as Pulcinella; the Davidsons were Pierrot and Pierette; and Miss Courtenay, of course, was Columbine. Now, quite early in the evening it was apparent that there was something wrong. Lord Cronshaw was moody and strange in his manner. When the party met together for supper in a small private room engaged by the host, everyone noticed that he and Miss Courtenay were no longer on speaking terms. She had obviously been crying, and seemed on the verge of hysterics. The meal was an uncomfortable one, and as they all left the supper room, she turned to Chris Davidson and requested him audibly to take her home, as she was 'sick of the ball.' The young actor hesitated, glancing at Lord Cronshaw, and finally drew them both back to the supper room.

"But all his efforts to secure a reconciliation were unavailing, and he accordingly got a taxi and escorted the now weeping Miss Courtenay back to her flat. Although obviously very much upset, she did not confide in him, merely reiterating again and again that she would 'make old

Cronch sorry for this!' That is the only hint we have that her death might not have been accidental, and it's precious little to go upon. By the time Davidson had quieted her down somewhat, it was too late to return to the Colossus Hall, and Davidson accordingly went straight home to his flat in Chelsea, where his wife arrived shortly afterwards, bearing the news of the terrible tragedy that had occurred after his departure.

"Lord Cronshaw, it seems, became more and more moody as the ball went on. He kept away from his party, and they hardly saw him during the rest of the evening. It was about one- thirty a.m ., just before the grand cotillion when everyone was to unmask, that Captain Digby, a brother officer who knew his disguise, noticed him standing in a box gazing down on the scene.

" 'Hullo, Cronch!' he called. 'Come down and be sociable! What are you moping about up there for like a boiled owl? Come along; there's a good old rag coming on now.'

" 'Right!' responded Cronshaw. 'Wait for me, or I'll never find you in the crowd.'

"He turned and left the box as he spoke. Captain Digby, who had Mrs. Davidson with him, waited. The minutes passed, but Lord Cronshaw did not appear. Finally Digby grew impatient.

" 'Does the fellow think we're going to wait all night for him?' he exclaimed. "At that moment Mrs. Mallaby joined them, and they explained the situation.

" 'Say, now,' cried the pretty widow vivaciously, 'he's like a bear with a sore head tonight.

Let's go right away and rout him out.'

"The search commenced, but met with no success until it occurred to Mrs. Mallaby that he might possibly be found in the room where they had supped an hour earlier. They made their way there. What a sight met their eyes! There was Harlequin, sure enough, but stretched on the ground with a table-knife in his heart!"

Japp stopped, and Poirot nodded, and said with the relish of the specialist: "Une belle affaire! And there was no clue as to the perpetrator of the deed? But how should there be!"

"Well," continued the inspector, "you know the rest. The tragedy was a double one. Next day there were headlines in all the papers, and a brief statement to the effect that Miss Courtenay, the popular actress, had been discovered dead in her bed, and that her death was due to an overdose of cocaine. Now, was it accident or suicide? Her maid, who was called upon to give evidence, admitted that Miss Courtenay was a confirmed taker of the drug, and a verdict of accidental death was returned. Nevertheless we can't leave the possibility of suicide out of account. Her death is particularly unfortunate, since it leaves us no clue now to the cause of the quarrel the preceding night. By the way, a small enamel box was found on the dead man. It had Coco written across it in diamonds, and was half full of cocaine. It was identified by Miss Courtenay's maid as belonging to her mistress, who nearly always carried it about with her, since it contained her supply of the drug to which she was fast becoming a slave."

"Was Lord Cronshaw himself addicted to the drug?"

"Very far from it. He held unusually strong views on the subject of dope." Poirot nodded thoughtfully.

"But since the box was in his possession, he knew that Miss Courtenay took it. Suggestive, that, is it not, my good Japp?"

"Ah!" said Japp rather vaguely. I smiled.

"Well," said Japp, "that's the case. What do you think of it?" "You found no clue of any kind that has not been reported?"

"Yes, there was this." Japp took a small object from his pocket and handed it over to Poirot. It was a small pompon of emerald green silk, with some ragged threads hanging from it, as

though it had been wrenched violently away.

"We found it in the dead man's hand, which was tightly clenched over it," explained the inspector.

Poirot handed it back without any comment and asked: "Had Lord Cronshaw any enemies?" "None that anyone knows of. He seemed a popular young fellow."

"Who benefits by his death?"

"His uncle, the Honourable Eustace Beltane, comes into the title and estates. There are one or two suspicious facts against him. Several people declare that they heard a violent altercation going on in the little supper room, and that Eustace Beltane was one of the disputants. You see, the table-knife being snatched up off the table would fit in with the murder being done in the heat of a quarrel."

"What does Mr. Beltane say about the matter?"

"Declares one of the waiters was the worse for liquor, and that he was giving him a dressing down. Also that it was nearer to one than half past. You see, Captain Digby's evidence fixes the time pretty accurately. Only about ten minutes elapsed between his speaking to Cronshaw and the finding of the body."

"And in any case I suppose Mr. Beltane, as Punchinello, was wearing a hump and a ruffle?" "I don't know the exact details of the costumes," said Japp, looking curiously at Poirot.

"And anyway, I don't quite see what that has got to do with it?"

"No?" There was a hint of mockery in Poirot's smile. He continued quietly, his eyes shining with the green light I had learned to recognize so well: "There was a curtain in this little supper room, was there not?"

"Yes, but—"

"With a space behind it sufficient to conceal a man?"

"Yes—in fact, there's a small recess, but how you knew about it—you haven't been to the place, have you, Monsieur Poirot?"

"No, my good Japp, I supplied the curtain from my brain. Without it, the drama is not reasonable. And always one must be reasonable. But tell me, did they not send for a doctor?"

"At once, of course. But there was nothing to be done. Death must have been instantaneous."

Poirot nodded rather impatiently.

"Yes, yes, I understand. This doctor, now, he gave evidence at the inquest?" "Yes."

"Did he say nothing of any unusual symptom—was there nothing about the appearance of the body which struck him as being abnormal?"

Japp stared hard at the little man.

"Yes, Monsieur Poirot. I don't know what you're getting at, but he did mention that there was a tension and stiffness about the limbs which he was quite at a loss to account for."

"Aha!" said Poirot. "Aha! Mon Dieu! Japp, that gives one to think, does it not?" I saw that it had certainly not given Japp to think.

"If you're thinking of poison, monsieur, who on earth would poison a man first and then stick a knife into him?"

"In truth that would be ridiculous," agreed Poirot placidly.

"Now is there anything you want to see, monsieur? If you'd like to examine the room where the body was found—"

Poirot waved his hand.

"Not in the least. You have told me the only thing that interests me—Lord Cronshaw's views on the subject of drug taking."

"Then there's nothing you want to see?" "Just one thing."

"What is that?"

"The set of china figures from which the costumes were copied." Japp stared.

"Well, you're a funny one!" "You can manage that for me?"

"Come round to Berkeley Square now if you like. Mr. Beltane—or His Lordship, as I should say now—won't object."

## II

We set off at once in a taxi. The new Lord Cronshaw was not at home, but at Japp's request we were shown into the "china room," where the gems of the collection were kept. Japp looked round him rather helplessly.

"I don't see how you'll ever find the ones you want, monsieur."

But Poirot had already drawn a chair in front of the mantelpiece and was hopping up upon it like a nimble robin. Above the mirror, on a small shelf to themselves, stood six china figures. Poirot examined them minutely, making a few comments to us as he did so.

The China Figures

"Les voilà! The old Italian Comedy. Three pairs! Harlequin and Columbine, Pierrot and Pierrette—very dainty in white and green—and Punchinello and Pulcinella in mauve and yellow. Very elaborate, the costume of Punchinello—ruffles and frills, a hump, a high hat. Yes, as I thought, very elaborate."

He replaced the figures carefully, and jumped down.

Japp looked unsatisfied, but as Poirot had clearly no intention of explaining anything, the detective put the best face he could upon the matter. As we were preparing to leave, the master of the house came in, and Japp performed the necessary introductions.

The sixth Viscount Cronshaw was a man of about fifty, suave in manner, with a handsome, dissolute face. Evidently an elderly roué, with the languid manner of a poseur. I took an instant dislike to him. He greeted us graciously enough, declaring he had heard great accounts of Poirot's skill, and placing himself at our disposal in every way.

"The police are doing all they can, I know," Poirot said.

"But I much fear the mystery of my nephew's death will never be cleared up. The whole thing seems utterly mysterious."

Poirot was watching him keenly. "Your nephew had no enemies that you know of?"

"None whatever. I am sure of that." He paused, and then went on: "If there are any questions you would like to ask—"

"Only one." Poirot's voice was serious. "The costumes—they were reproduced exactly from your figurines?"

"To the smallest detail."

"Thank you, milor'. That is all I wanted to be sure of. I wish you good day."

"And what next?" inquired Japp as we hurried down the street. "I've got to report at the Yard, you know."

"Bien! I will not detain you. I have one other little matter to attend to, and then—"

"Yes?"

"The case will be complete."

"What? You don't mean it! You know who killed Lord Cronshaw?"

"Parfaitement."

"Who was it? Eustace Beltane?"

"Ah, mon ami, you know my little weakness! Always I have a desire to keep the threads in my own hands up to the last minute. But have no fear. I will reveal all when the time comes. I want no credit—the affair shall be yours, on the condition that you permit me to play out the dénouement my own way."

"That's fair enough," said Japp. "That is, if the dénouement ever comes! But I say, you are

an oyster, aren't you?" Poirot smiled. "Well, so long. I'm off to the Yard." He strode off down the steet, and Poirot hailed a passing taxi. "Where are we going now?" I asked in lively curiosity.

"To Chelsea to see the Davidsons." He gave the address to the driver.

"What do you think of the new Lord Cronshaw?" I asked. "What says my good friend Hastings?"

"I distrust him instinctively."

"You think he is the 'wicked uncle' of the storybooks, eh?" "Don't you?"

"Me, I think he was most amiable towards us," said Poirot noncommittally. "Because he had his reasons!"

Poirot looked at me, shook his head sadly, and murmured something that sounded like: "No method."

The Davidsons lived on the third floor of a block of "mansion" flats. Mr. Davidson was out, we were told, but Mrs. Davidson was at home. We were ushered into a long, low room with garish Oriental hangings. The air felt close and oppressive, and there was an overpowering fragrance of joss sticks. Mrs. Davidson came to us almost immediately, a small, fair creature whose fragility would have seemed pathetic and appealing had it not been for the rather shrewd and calculating gleam in her light blue eyes.

Poirot explained our connection with the case, and she shook her head sadly.

"Poor Cronch—and poor Coco too! We were both so fond of her, and her death has been a terrible grief to us. What is it you want to ask me? Must I really go over all that dreadful evening again?"

"Oh, madame, believe me, I would not harass your feelings unnecessarily. Indeed, Inspector Japp has told me all that is needful. I only wish to see the costume you wore at the ball that night."

The lady looked somewhat surprised, and Poirot continued smoothly: "You comprehend, madame, that I work on the system of my country. There we always 'reconstruct' the crime. It is possible that I may have an actual représentation, and if so, you understand, the costumes would be important."

Mrs. Davidson still looked a bit doubtful.

"I've heard of reconstructing a crime, of course," she said. "But I didn't know you were so

particular about details. But I'll fetch the dress now."

She left the room and returned almost immediately with a dainty wisp of white satin and green. Poirot took it from her and examined it, handing it back with a bow.

"Merci, madame! I see you have had the misfortune to lose one of your green pompons, the one on the shoulder here."

"Yes, it got torn off at the ball. I picked it up and gave it to poor Lord Cronshaw to keep for

me."

"That was after supper?" "Yes."

"Not long before the tragedy, perhaps?"

A faint look of alarm came into Mrs. Davidson's pale eyes, and she replied quickly: "Oh no

—long before that. Quite soon after supper, in fact."

"I see. Well, that is all. I will not derange you further. Bonjour, madame."

"Well," I said as we emerged from the building, "that explains the mystery of the green pompon."

"I wonder."

"Why, what do you mean?"

"You saw me examine the dress, Hastings?" "Yes?"

"Eh bien, the pompon that was missing had not been wrenched off, as the lady said. On the contrary, it had been cut off, my friend, cut off with scissors. The threads were all quite even."

"Dear me!" I exclaimed. "This becomes more and more involved."

"On the contrary," replied Poirot placidly, "it becomes more and more simple."

"Poirot," I cried, "one day I shall murder you! Your habit of finding everything perfectly simple is aggravating to the last degree!"

"But when I explain, mon ami, is it not always perfectly simple?"

"Yes; that is the annoying part of it! I feel then that I could have done it myself."

"And so you could, Hastings, so you could. If you would but take the trouble of arranging your ideas! Without method—"

"Yes, yes," I said hastily, for I knew Poirot's eloquence when started on his favourite theme only too well. "Tell me, what do we do next? Are you really going to reconstruct the crime?"

"Hardly that. Shall we say that the drama is over, but that I propose to add a— harlequinade?"

Captain Arthur Hastings

## IV

The following Tuesday was fixed upon by Poirot as the day for this mysterious performance. The preparations greatly intrigued me. A white screen was erected at one side of the room, flanked by heavy curtains at either side. A man with some lighting apparatus arrived next, and finally a group of members of the theatrical profession, who disappeared into Poirot's bedroom, which had been rigged up as a temporary dressing room.

Shortly before eight, Japp arrived, in no very cheerful mood. I gathered that the official detective hardly approved of Poirot's plan.

"Bit melodramatic, like all his ideas. But there, it can do no harm, and as he says, it might save us a good bit of trouble. He's been very smart over the case. I was on the same scent myself, of course—" I felt instinctively that Japp was straining the truth here— "but there, I

promised to let him play the thing out his own way. Ah! Here is the crowd."

His Lordship arrived first, escorting Mrs. Mallaby, whom I had not as yet seen. She was a pretty, dark-haired woman, and appeared perceptibly nervous. The Davidsons followed. Chris Davidson also I saw for the first time. He was hand-some enough in a rather obvious style, tall and dark, with the easy grace of the actor.

Poirot had arranged seats for the party facing the screen. This was illuminated by a bright light. Poirot switched out the other lights so that the room was in darkness except for the screen. Poirot's voice rose out of the gloom.

"Messieurs, mesdames, a word of explanation. Six figures in turn will pass across the screen. They are familiar to you. Pierrot and his Pierrette; Punchinello the buffoon, and elegant Pulcinella; beautiful Columbine, lightly dancing, Harlequin, the sprite, invisible to man!"

Punchinello the buffoon

With these words of introduction, the show began. In turn each figure that Poirot had mentioned bounded before the screen, stayed there a moment poised, and then vanished. The lights went up, and a sigh of relief went round.

Everyone had been nervous, fearing they knew not what. It seemed to me that the proceedings had gone singularly flat. If the criminal was among us, and Poirot expected him to break down at the mere sight of a familiar figure the device had failed signally—as it was almost bound to do. Poirot, however, appeared not a whit discomposed. He stepped forward, beaming.

"Now, messieurs and mesdames, will you be so good as to tell me, one at a time, what it is that we have just seen? Will you begin, milor'?"

The gentleman looked rather puzzled. "I'm afraid I don't quite understand." "Just tell me what we have been seeing."

"I—er—well, I should say we have seen six figures passing in front of a screen and dressed to represent the personages in the old Italian Comedy, or—er—ourselves the other night."

"Never mind the other night, milor'," broke in Poirot. "The first part of your speech was what I wanted. Madame, you agree with Milor' Cronshaw?"

He had turned as he spoke to Mrs. Mallaby. "I—er—yes, of course."

"You agree that you have seen six figures representing the Italian Comedy?" "Why, certainly."

"Monsieur Davidson? You too?" "Yes."

"Madame?"

"Yes."

"Hastings? Japp? Yes? You are all in accord?"

He looked around upon us; his face grew rather pale, and his eyes were green as any cat's. "And yet—you are all wrong! Your eyes have lied to you—as they lied to you on the night

of the Victory Ball. To 'see' things with your eyes, as they say, is not always to see the truth. One must see with the eyes of the mind; one must employ the little cells of grey! Know, then, that tonight and on the night of the Victory Ball, you saw not six figures but five! See!"

The lights went out again. A figure bounded in front of the screen—Pierrot!

"Who is that?" demanded Poirot. "Is it Pierrot?"

"Yes," we all cried. "Look again!"

With a swift movement the man divested himself of his loose Pierrot garb. There in the limelight stood glittering Harlequin! At the same moment there was a cry and an overturned

chair.

"Curse you," snarled Davidson's voice. "Curse you! How did you guess?"

Then came the clink of handcuffs and Japp's calm official voice. "I arrest you, Christopher Davidson—charge of murdering Viscount Cronshaw—anything you say will be used in evidence against you."

## V

It was a quarter of an hour later. A recherché little supper had appeared; and Poirot, beaming all over his face, was dispensing hospitality and answering our eager questions.

"It was all very simple. The circumstances in which the green pompon was found suggested at once that it had been torn from the costume of the murderer. I dismissed Pierrette from my mind (since it takes considerable strength to drive a table-knife home) and fixed upon Pierrot as the criminal. But Pierrot left the ball nearly two hours before the murder was committed. So he must either have returned to the ball later to kill Lord Cronshaw, or—eh bien, he must have killed him before he left! Was that impossible? Who had seen Lord Cronshaw after supper that evening? Only Mrs. Davidson, whose statement, I suspected, was a deliberate fabrication uttered with the object of accounting for the missing pompon, which, of course, she cut from her own dress to replace the one missing on her husband's costume. But then, Harlequin, who was seen in the box at one-thirty, must have been an impersonation. For a moment, earlier, I had considered the possibility of Mr. Beltane being the guilty party. But with his elaborate costume, it was clearly impossible that he could have doubled the roles of Punchinello and Harlequin. On the other hand, to Davidson, a young man of about the same height as the murdered man and an actor by profession, the thing was simplicity itself.

"But one thing worried me. Surely a doctor could not fail to perceive the difference between a man who had been dead two hours and one who had been dead ten minutes! Eh bien, the doctor did perceive it! But he was not taken to the body and asked, "How long has this man been dead?" On the contrary, he was informed that the man had been seen alive ten minutes ago, and so he merely commented at the inquest on the abnormal stiffening of the limbs for which he was quite unable to account!

"All was now marching famously for my theory. Davidson had killed Lord Cronshaw immediately after supper, when, as you remember, he was seen to draw him back into the supper room. Then he departed with Miss Courtenay, left her at the door of her flat (instead of going in and trying to pacify her as he affirmed) and returned posthaste to the Colossus—but as Harlequin, not Pierrot—a simple transformation effected by removing his outer costume."

## VI

The uncle of the dead man leaned forward, his eyes perplexed.

"But if so, he must have come to the ball prepared to kill his victim. What earthly motive could he have had? The motive, that's what I can't get."

"Ah! There we come to the second tragedy—that of Miss Courtenay. There was one simple point which everyone overlooked. Miss Courtenay died of cocaine poisoning—but her supply of the drug was in the enamel box which was found on Lord Cronshaw's body. Where, then, did she obtain the dose which killed her? Only one person could have supplied her with it— Davidson. And that explains everything. It accounts for her friendship with the Davidsons and

her demand that Davidson should escort her home. Lord Cronshaw, who was almost fanatically opposed to drug-taking, discovered that she was addicted to cocaine, and suspected that Davidson supplied her with it. Davidson doubtless denied this, but Lord Cronshaw determined to get the truth from Miss Courtenay at the ball. He could forgive the wretched girl, but he would certainly have no mercy on the man who made a living by trafficking in drugs. Exposure and ruin confronted Davidson. He went to the ball determined that Cronshaw's silence must be obtained at any cost."

"Was Coco's death an accident, then?"

"I suspect that it was an accident cleverly engineered by Davidson. She was furiously angry with Cronshaw, first for his reproaches, and secondly for taking her cocaine from her. Davidson supplied her with more, and probably suggested her augmenting the dose as a defiance to 'old Cronch!' "

"One other thing," I said. "The recess and the curtain? How did you know about them?" "Why, mon ami, that was the most simple of all. Waiters had been in and out of that little

room, so, obviously, the body could not have been lying where it was found on the floor. There must be some place in the room where it could be hidden. I deduced a curtain and a recess behind it. Davidson dragged the body there, and later, after drawing attention to himself in the box, he dragged it out again before finally leaving the Hall. It was one of his best moves. He is a clever fellow!"

But in Poirot's green eyes I read unmistakably the unspoken remark: "But not quite so clever as Hercule Poirot!"

# Chapter 3

# The Red Signal

'No, but how too thrilling,' said pretty Mrs Eversleigh, opening her lovely, but slightly vacant eyes very wide. 'They always say women have a sixth sense; do you think it's true, Sir Alington?'

The famous alienist smiled sardonically. He had an unbounded contempt for the foolish pretty type, such as his fellow guest. Alington West was the supreme authority on mental disease, and he was fully alive to his own position and importance. A slightly pompous man of full figure.

'A great deal of nonsense is talked, I know that, Mrs Eversleigh. What does the term mean—a sixth sense?'

'You scientific men are always so severe. And it really is extraordinary the way one seems to positively know things sometimes—just know them, feel them, I mean—quite uncanny—it really is. Claire knows what I mean, don't you, Claire?'

She appealed to her hostess with a slight pout, and a tilted shoulder.

Claire Trent did not reply at once. It was a small dinner party, she and her husband, Violet Eversleigh, Sir Alington West, and his nephew, Dermot West, who was an old friend of Jack Trent's. Jack Trent himself, a somewhat heavy florid man, with a good-humoured smile, and a pleasant lazy laugh, took up the thread.

'Bunkum, Violet! Your best friend is killed in a railway accident. Straight away you remember that you dreamt of a black cat last Tuesday—marvellous, you felt all

along that something was going to happen!'

'Oh, no, Jack, you're mixing up premoni-
tions with intuition now. Come, now, Sir
Alington, you must admit that premoni-
tions are real?'

'To a certain extent, perhaps,' admitted the physician cautiously. 'But coincidence accounts for a good deal, and
then there is the invariable tendency
to make the most of a story afterwards—you've always got to take that
into account.'

'I don't think there is any such thing as premonition,' said Claire Trent, rather abruptly. 'Or intuition, or a sixth sense, or any of the things we talk about so glibly. We go through life like a train rushing through the darkness to an un-known destination.'

'That's hardly a good simile, Mrs Trent,' said Dermot West, lifting his head for the first time and taking part in the discussion. There was a curious glitter in the clear grey eyes that shone out rather oddly from the deeply tanned face. 'You've forgotten the signals, you see.'

'The signals?'

'Yes, green if it's all right, and red—for danger!'

'Red—for danger—how thrilling!' breathed Violet Eversleigh.

Dermot turned from her rather impatiently.

'That's just a way of describing it, of course. Danger ahead! The red signal! Look out!'

Trent stared at him curiously.

'You speak as though it were an actual experience, Dermot, old boy.'

'So it is—has been, I mean.'

'Give us the yarn.'

'I can give you one instance. Out in Mesopotamia—just after the Armistice, I came into my tent one evening with the feeling strong upon me. Danger! Look out! Hadn't the ghost of a notion what it was all about. I made a round of the camp, fussed unnecessarily, took all precautions against an attack by hostile Arabs. Then I went back to my tent. As soon as I got inside, the feeling popped up again stronger than ever. Danger! In the end, I took a blanket outside, rolled myself up in it and slept there.'

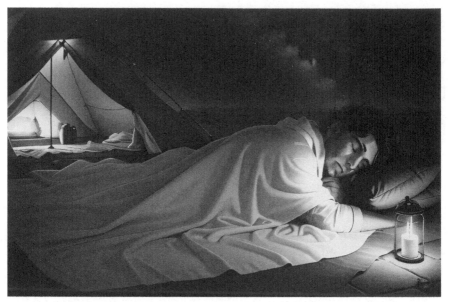

Dermot sleeping outside his tent

'Well?'

'The next morning, when I went inside the tent, first thing I saw was a great knife arrangement—about half a yard long—struck down through my bunk, just where I would have lain. I soon found out about it—one of the Arab servants. His son had been shot as a spy. What have you got to say to that, Uncle Alington, as an example of what I call the red signal?'

The specialist smiled non-committally.

'A very interesting story, my dear Dermot.'

'But not one that you would accept unreservedly?'

'Yes, yes, I have no doubt that you had the premonition of danger, just as you state. But it is the origin of the premonition I dispute. According to you, it came from without, impressed by some outside source upon your mentality. But nowadays we find that nearly everything comes from within—from our subconscious self.'

'Good old subconscious,' cried Jack Trent. 'It's the jack-of-all-trades nowadays.'

Sir Alington continued without heeding the interruption.

'I suggest that by some glance or look this Arab had betrayed himself. Your conscious self did not notice or remember, but with your subconscious self it was otherwise. The subconscious never forgets. We believe, too, that it can reason and deduce quite independently of the higher or conscious will. Your subconscious self, then, believed that an attempt might be made to assassinate you, and succeeded in forcing its fear upon your conscious realization.'

'That sounds very convincing, I admit,' said Dermot, smiling.

'But not nearly so exciting,' pouted Mrs Eversleigh.

'It is also possible that you may have been subconsciously aware of the hate felt by the man towards you. What in old days used to be called telepathy certainly exists, though the conditions governing it are very little understood.'

'Have there been any other instances?' asked Claire of Dermot.

'Oh! yes, but nothing very pictorial—and I suppose they could all be explained under the heading of coincidence. I refused an invitation to a country house once, for no other reason than the hoisting of the "red signal". The place was burnt out during the week. By the way, Uncle Alington, where does the subconscious come in there?'

'I'm afraid it doesn't,' said Alington, smiling.

'But you've got an equally good explanation. Come, now. No need to be tactful with near relatives.'

'Well, then, nephew, I venture to suggest that you refused the invitation for the ordinary reason that you didn't much want to go, and that after the fire, you suggested to yourself that you had had a warning of danger, which explanation you now believe implicitly.'

'It's hopeless,' laughed Dermot. 'It's heads you win, tails I lose.'

'Never mind, Mr West,' cried Violet Eversleigh. 'I believe in your Red Signal implicitly. Is the time in Mesopotamia the last time you had it?'

'Yes—until—'

'I beg your pardon?'

'Nothing.'

Dermot sat silent. The words which had nearly left his lips were: 'Yes, until tonight.' They had come quite unbidden to his lips, voicing a thought which had as yet not been consciously realized, but he was aware at once that they were true. The Red Signal was looming up out of the darkness. Danger! Danger close at hand!

But why? What conceivable danger could there be here? Here in the house of his friends? At least—well, yes, there was that kind of danger. He looked at Claire Trent—her whiteness, her slenderness, the exquisite droop of her golden head. But that danger had been there for some time—it was never likely to get acute. For Jack Trent was his best friend, and more than his best friend, the man who had saved his life in Flanders and had been recommended for the VC for doing so. A good fellow, Jack, one of the best. Damned bad luck that he should have fallen in love with Jack's wife. He'd get over it some day, he supposed. A thing couldn't go on hurting like this for ever. One could starve it out—that was it, starve it out. It was not as though she would ever guess—and if she did guess, there was no danger of her caring. A statue, a beautiful statue, a thing of gold and ivory and pale pink coral . . . a toy for a king, not a real woman . . .

Claire . . . the very thought of her name, uttered silently, hurt him . . . He must get over it. He'd cared for women before . . . 'But not like this!' said something. 'Not like this.' Well, there it was. No danger there—heartache, yes, but not danger. Not the danger of the Red Signal. That was for something else.

He looked round the table and it struck him for the first time that it was rather an unusual little gathering. His uncle, for instance, seldom dined out in this small, informal way. It was not as though the Trents were old friends; until this evening Dermot had not been aware that he knew them at all.

To be sure, there was an excuse. A rather notorious medium was coming after dinner to give a séance. Sir Alington professed to be mildly interested in spiritualism. Yes, that was an excuse, certainly.

The word forced itself on his notice. An excuse. Was the séance just an excuse to make the specialist's presence at dinner natural? If so, what was the real object of his being here? A host of details came rushing into Dermot's mind, trifles unnoticed at the time, or, as his uncle would have said, unnoticed by the conscious mind.

The great physician had looked oddly, very oddly, at Claire more than once. He seemed to be watching her. She was uneasy under his scrutiny. She made little twitching motions with her hands. She was nervous, horribly nervous, and was it, could it be, frightened? Why was she frightened?

With a jerk, he came back to the conversation round the table. Mrs Eversleigh had got the great man talking upon his own subject.

'My dear lady,' he was saying, 'what is madness? I can assure you that the more we study the subject, the more difficult we find it to pronounce. We all practise a certain amount of self-deception, and when we carry it so far as to believe we are the Czar of Russia, we are shut up or restrained. But there is a long road before we reach that point. At what particular spot on it shall we erect a post and say, "On this side sanity, on the other madness?" It can't be done, you know. And I will tell you this, if the man suffering from a delusion happened to hold his tongue about it, in all probability we should never be able to distinguish him from a normal individual. The extraordinary sanity of the insane is a most interesting subject.'

Sir Alington sipped his wine with appreciation, and beamed upon the company.

'I've always heard they are very cunning,' remarked Mrs Eversleigh. 'Loonies, I mean.'

'Remarkably so. And suppression of one's particular delusion has a disastrous effect very often. All suppressions are dangerous, as psychoanalysis has taught us. The man who has a harmless eccentricity, and can indulge it as such, seldom goes over the border line. But the man'—he paused—'or woman who is to all appearance perfectly normal may be in reality a poignant source of danger to the community.'

His gaze travelled gently down the table to Claire, and then back again. He sipped his wine once more.

A horrible fear shook Dermot. Was that what he meant? Was that what he was driving at? Impossible, but—

'And all from suppressing oneself,' sighed Mrs Eversleigh. 'I quite see that one should be very careful always to—to express one's personality. The dangers of the other are frightful.'

'My dear Mrs Eversleigh,' expostulated the physician. 'You have quite misunderstood me. The cause of the mischief is in the physical matter of the brain—sometimes arising from some outward agency such as a blow; sometimes, alas, congenital.'

'Heredity is so sad,' sighed the lady vaguely. 'Consumption and all that.'

'Tuberculosis is not hereditary,' said Sir Alington drily.

'Isn't it? I always thought it was. But madness is! How dreadful. What else?'

'Gout,' said Sir Alington smiling. 'And colour blindness—the latter is rather interesting. It is transmitted direct to males, but is latent in females. So, while there are many colour-blind men, for a woman to be colour-blind, it must have been latent in her mother as well as present in her father—rather an unusual state of things to occur. That is what is called sex-limited heredity.'

'How interesting. But madness is not like that, is it?'

'Madness can be handed down to men or women equally,' said the physician gravely.

Claire rose suddenly, pushing back her chair so abruptly that it overturned and fell to the ground. She was very pale and the nervous motions of her fingers were very apparent.

'You—you will not be long, will you?' she begged. 'Mrs Thompson will be here in a few minutes now.'

'One glass of port, and I will be with you, for one,' declared Sir Alington. 'To see this wonderful Mrs Thompson's performance is what I have come for, is it not? Ha, ha! Not that I needed any inducement.' He bowed.

Claire gave a faint smile of acknowledg-
ment and passed out of the room, her
hand on Mrs Eversleigh's shoulder.

'Afraid I've been talking shop,' remarked
the physician as he resumed his seat.
'Forgive me, my dear fellow.'

'Not at all,' said Trent perfunctorily.

He looked strained and worried. For the
first time Dermot felt an outsider in the
company of his friend. Between these
two was a secret that even an old friend
might not share. And yet the whole thing
was fantastic and incredible. What had

he to go upon? Nothing but a couple of glances and a woman's nervousness.

They lingered over their wine but a very short time, and arrived up in the drawing-room just as Mrs Thompson was announced.

The medium was a plump middle-aged woman, atrociously dressed in magenta velvet, with a loud rather common voice.

'Hope I'm not late, Mrs Trent,' she said cheerily. 'You did say nine o'clock, didn't you?'

'You are quite punctual, Mrs Thompson,' said Claire in her sweet, slightly husky voice. 'This is our little circle.'

No further introductions were made, as was evidently the custom. The medium swept them all with a shrewd, penetrating eye.

'I hope we shall get some good results,' she remarked briskly. 'I can't tell you how I hate it when I go out and I can't give satisfaction, so to speak. It just makes me mad. But I think Shiromako (my Japanese control, you know) will be able to get through all right tonight. I'm feeling ever so fit, and I refused the welsh rabbit, fond of toasted cheese though I am.'

Dermot listened, half amused, half disgusted. How prosaic the whole thing was! And yet, was he not judging foolishly? Everything, after all, was natural—the powers claimed by mediums were natural powers, as yet imperfectly understood. A great surgeon might be wary of indigestion on the eve of a delicate operation. Why not Mrs Thompson?

Chairs were arranged in a circle, lights so that they could conveniently be raised or lowered. Dermot noticed that there was no question of tests, or of Sir Alington satisfying himself as to the conditions of the séance. No, this business of Mrs Thompson was only a blind. Sir Alington was here for quite another purpose. Claire's mother, Dermot remembered, had died abroad. There had been some mystery about her . . . Hereditary . . .

With a jerk he forced his mind back to the surroundings of the moment.

Everyone took their places, and the lights were turned out, all but a small red-shaded one on a far table.

Seance room

For a while nothing was heard but the low even breathing of the medium. Gradually it grew more and more stertorous. Then, with a suddenness that made Dermot jump, a loud rap came from the far end of the room. It was repeated from the other side. Then a perfect crescendo of raps was heard. They died away, and a sudden high peal of mocking laughter rang through the room. Then silence, broken by a voice utterly unlike that of Mrs Thompson, a high-pitched quaintly inflected voice.

'I am here, gentlemen,' it said. 'Yess, I am here. You wish to ask me things?'

'Who are you? Shiromako?'

'Yess. I Shiromako. I pass over long time ago. I work. I very happy.'

Further details of Shiromako's life followed. It was all very flat and uninteresting, and Dermot had heard it often before. Everyone was happy, very happy.

Messages were given from vaguely described relatives, the description being so loosely worded as to fit almost any contingency. An elderly lady, the mother of someone present, held the floor for some time, imparting copy book maxims with an air of refreshing novelty hardly borne out by her subject matter.

'Someone else want to get through now,' announced Shiromako. 'Got a very important message for one of the gentlemen.'

There was a pause, and then a new voice spoke, prefacing its remark with an evil demoniacal chuckle.

'Ha, ha! Ha, ha, ha! Better not go home. Better not go home. Take my advice.'

'Who are you speaking to?' asked Trent.

'One of you three. I shouldn't go home if I were him. Danger! Blood! Not very much blood—quite enough. No, don't go home.' The voice grew fainter. 'Don't go home!'

It died away completely. Dermot felt his blood tingling. He was convinced that the warning was meant for him. Somehow or other, there was danger abroad tonight.

There was a sigh from the medium, and then a groan. She was coming round. The lights were turned on, and presently she sat upright, her eyes blinking a little.

'Go off well, my dear? I hope so.'

'Very good indeed, thank you, Mrs Thompson.'

The medium Mrs. Thompson

'Shiromako, I suppose?'


'Yes, and others.'


Mrs Thompson yawned.

'I'm dead beat. Absolutely down and out. Does fairly take it out of you. Well, I'm glad it was a success. I was a bit afraid it mightn't be—afraid something disagreeable might happen. There's a queer feel about this room tonight.'

She glanced over each ample shoulder in turn, and then shrugged them uncomfortably.

'I don't like it,' she said. 'Any sudden deaths among any of you people lately?'

'What do you mean—among us?'

'Near relatives—dear friends? No? Well, if I wanted to be melodramatic, I'd say there was death in the air tonight. There, it's only my nonsense. Goodbye, Mrs Trent. I'm glad you've been satisfied.'

Mrs Thompson in her magenta velvet gown went out.

'I hope you've been interested, Sir Alington,' murmured Claire.

'A most interesting evening, my dear lady. Many thanks for the opportunity. Let me wish you good night. You are all going to a dance, are you not?'

'Won't you come with us?'

'No, no. I make it a rule to be in bed by half past eleven. Good night. Good night, Mrs Eversleigh. Ah! Dermot, I rather want to have a word with you. Can you come with me now? You can rejoin the others at the Grafton Galleries.'

'Certainly, uncle. I'll meet you there then, Trent.'

Very few words were exchanged between uncle and nephew during the short drive to Harley Street. Sir Alington made a semi-apology for dragging

Dermot away, and assured him that he would only detain him a few minutes.

'Shall I keep the car for you, my boy?' he asked, as they alighted.

'Oh, don't bother, uncle. I'll pick up a taxi.'

'Very good. I don't like to keep Charlson up later than I can help. Good night, Charlson. Now where the devil did I put my key?'

The car glided away as Sir Alington stood on the steps vainly searching his pockets.

'Must have left it in my other coat,' he said at length. 'Ring the bell, will you? Johnson is still up, I dare say.'

The imperturbable Johnson did indeed open the door within sixty seconds.

'Mislaid my key, Johnson,' explained Sir Alington. 'Bring a couple of whiskies and sodas into the library, will you?'

'Very good, Sir Alington.'

The physician strode on into the library and turned on the lights. He motioned to Dermot to close the door behind him after entering.

'I won't keep you long, Dermot, but there's just something I want to say to you. Is it my fancy, or have you a certain—tendresse, shall we say, for Mrs Jack Trent?'

The blood rushed to Dermot's face.

'Jack Trent is my best friend.'

'Pardon me, but that is hardly answering my question. I dare say that you consider my views on divorce and such matters highly puritanical, but I must remind you that you are my only near relative and that you are my heir.'

'There is no question of a divorce,' said Dermot angrily.

'There certainly is not, for a reason which I understand perhaps better than you do. That particular reason I cannot give you now, but I do wish to warn you. Claire Trent is not for you.'

The young man faced his uncle's gaze steadily.

'I do understand—and permit me to say, perhaps better than you think. I know the reason for your presence at dinner tonight.'

'Eh?' The physician was clearly startled. 'How did you know that?'

'Call it a guess, sir. I am right, am I not, when I say that you were there in your—professional capacity.'

Sir Alington strode up and down.

'You are quite right, Dermot. I could not, of course, have told you so myself, though I am afraid it will soon be common property.'

Dermot's heart contracted.

'You mean that you have—made up your mind?'

'Yes, there is insanity in the family—on the mother's side. A sad case—a very sad case.'

'I can't believe it, sir.'

'I dare say not. To the layman there are few if any signs apparent.'

'And to the expert?'

'The evidence is conclusive. In such a case, the patient must be placed under restraint as soon as possible.'

'My God!' breathed Dermot. 'But you can't shut anyone up for nothing at all.'

'My dear Dermot! Cases are only placed under restraint when their being at large would result in danger to the community.

'Danger?'

'Very grave danger. In all probability a peculiar form of homicidal mania. It was so in the mother's case.'

Dermot turned away with a groan, burying his face in his hands. Claire—white and golden Claire!

'In the circumstances,' continued the physician comfortably, 'I felt it incumbent on me to warn you.'

'Claire,' murmured Dermot. 'My poor Claire.'

'Yes, indeed, we must all pity her.'

Suddenly Dermot raised his head.

'I don't believe it.'

'What?'

'I say I don't believe it. Doctors make mistakes. Everyone knows that. And they're always keen on their own speciality.'

'My dear Dermot,' cried Sir Alington angrily.

'I tell you I don't believe it—and anyway, even if it is so, I don't care. I love Claire. If she will come with me, I shall take her away—far away—out of the reach of meddling physicians. I shall guard her, care for her, shelter her with my love.'

'You will do nothing of the sort. Are you mad?'

Dermot laughed scornfully.

'You would say so, I dare say.'

'Understand me, Dermot.' Sir Alington's face was red with suppressed passion. 'If you do this thing—this shameful thing—it is the end. I shall withdraw the allowance I am now making you, and I shall make a new will leaving all I possess to various hospitals.'

'Do as you please with your damned money,' said Dermot in a low voice. 'I shall have the woman I love.'

'A woman who—'

'Say a word against her, and, by God! I'll kill you!' cried Dermot.

A slight clink of glasses made them both swing round. Unheard by them in the heat of their argument, Johnson had entered with a tray of glasses. His face was the imperturbable one of the good servant, but Dermot wondered how much he had overheard.

'That'll do, Johnson,' said Sir Alington curtly. 'You can go to bed.'

'Thank you, sir. Good night, sir.'

Johnson withdrew.

The two men looked at each other. The momentary interruption had calmed the storm.

'Uncle,' said Dermot. 'I shouldn't have spoken to you as I did. I can quite see that from your point of view you are perfectly right. But I have loved Claire Trent for a long time. The fact that Jack Trent is my best friend has hitherto stood in the way of my ever speaking of love to Claire herself. But in these circumstances that fact no longer counts. The idea that any monetary conditions can deter me is absurd. I think we've both said all there is to be said. Good night.'

'Dermot—'

'It is really no good arguing further. Good night, Uncle Alington. I'm sorry, but there it is.'

He went out quickly, shutting the door behind him. The hall was in darkness. He passed through it, opened the front door and emerged into the street, banging the door behind him.

A taxi had just deposited a fare at a house farther along the street and Dermot hailed it, and drove to the Grafton Galleries.

In the door of the ballroom he stood for a minute bewildered, his head spinning. The raucous jazz music, the smiling women—it was as though he had stepped into another world.

Had he dreamt it all? Impossible that that grim conversation with his uncle should have really taken place. There was Claire floating past, like a lily in her white and silver gown that fitted sheath-like to her slenderness. She smiled at him, her face calm and serene. Surely it was all a dream.

The dance had stopped. Presently she was near him, smiling up into his face. As in a dream he asked her to dance.

She was in his arms now, the raucous melodies had begun again.

He felt her flag a little.

'Tired? Do you want to stop?'

'If you don't mind. Can we go some-where where we can talk? There is some-thing I want to say to you.'

Not a dream. He came back to earth with a bump. Could he ever have thought her face calm and serene? It was haunted with anxiety, with dread. How much did she know?

He found a quiet corner, and they sat down side by side.

'Well,' he said, assuming a lightness he did not feel. 'You said you had something you wanted to say to me?'

'Yes.' Her eyes were cast down. She was playing nervously with the tassel of her gown. 'It's difficult—rather.'

'Tell me, Claire.'

'It's just this. I want you to—to go away for a time.'

He was astonished. Whatever he had expected, it was not this.

'You want me to go away? Why?'

'It's best to be honest, isn't it? I—I know that you are a—a gentleman and my friend. I want you to go away because I—I have let myself get fond of you.'

'Claire.'

Her words left him dumb—tongue-tied.

'Please do not think that I am conceited enough to fancy that you—that you would ever be likely to fall in love with me. It is only that—I am not very happy—and—oh! I would rather you went away.'

'Claire, don't you know that I have cared—cared damnably—ever since I met you?'

She lifted startled eyes to his face.

'You cared? You have cared a long time?'

'Since the beginning.'

'Oh!' she cried. 'Why didn't you tell me? Then? When I could have come to you! Why tell me now when it's too late. No, I'm mad—I don't know what I'm saying. I could never have come to you.'

'Claire, what did you mean when you said "now that it's too late?" Is it—is it because of my uncle? What he knows? What he thinks?'

She nodded dumbly, the tears running down her face.

'Listen, Claire, you're not to believe all that. You're not to think about it. Instead you will come away with me. We'll go to the South Seas, to islands like green jewels. You will be happy there, and I will look after you—keep you safe for always.'

His arms went round her. He drew her to him, felt her tremble at his touch. Then suddenly she wrenched herself free.

'Oh, no, please. Can't you see? I couldn't now. It would be ugly—ugly—ugly. All along I've wanted to be good—and now—it would be ugly as well.'

He hesitated, baffled by her words. She looked at him appealingly.

'Please,' she said. 'I want to be good . . .'

Without a word, Dermot got up and left her. For the moment he was touched and racked by her words beyond argument. He went for his hat and coat, running into Trent as he did so.

'Hallo, Dermot, you're off early.'

'Yes, I'm not in the mood for dancing tonight.'

'It's a rotten night,' said Trent gloomily. 'But you haven't got my worries.'

Dermot had a sudden panic that Trent might be going to confide in him. Not that—anything but that!

'Well, so long,' he said hurriedly. 'I'm off home.'

'Home, eh? What about the warning of the spirits?'

'I'll risk that. Good night, Jack.'

Dermot's flat was not far away. He walked there, feeling the need of the cool night air to calm his fevered brain.

He let himself in with his key and switched on the light in the bedroom.

And all at once, for the second time that night, the feeling that he had designated by the title of the Red Signal surged over him. So overpowering was it that for the moment it swept even Claire from his mind.

Danger! He was in danger. At this very moment, in this very room, he was in danger.

He tried in vain to ridicule himself free of the fear. Perhaps his efforts were secretly half-hearted. So far, the Red Signal had given him timely warning which had enabled him to avoid disaster. Smiling a little at his own superstition, he made a careful tour of the flat. It was possible that some malefactor had got in and was lying concealed there. But his search revealed nothing. His man Milson, was away, and the flat was absolutely empty.

He returned to his bedroom and un-dressed slowly, frowning to himself. The sense of danger was acute as ever. He went to a drawer to get out a hand-kerchief, and suddenly stood stock still. There was an unfamiliar lump in the middle of the drawer—something hard.

His quick nervous fingers tore aside the handkerchiefs and took out the object concealed beneath them. It was a revolver.

With the utmost astonishment Dermot examined it keenly. It was of a somewhat unfamiliar pattern, and one shot had been fired from it lately. Beyond that, he could make nothing of it. Someone had placed it in that drawer that very evening. It had not been there when he dressed for dinner—he was sure of that.

He was about to replace it in the drawer, when he was startled by a bell ringing. It rang again and again, sounding unusually loud in the quietness of the empty flat.

Who could it be coming to the front door at this hour? And only one answer came to the question—an answer instinctive and persistent.

'Danger—danger—danger . . .'

Led by some instinct for which he did not account, Dermot switched off his light, slipped on an overcoat that lay across a chair, and opened the hall door.

Two men stood outside. Beyond them Dermot caught sight of a blue uniform. A policeman!

'Mr West?' asked the foremost of the two men.

It seemed to Dermot that ages elapsed before he answered. In reality it was only a few seconds before he replied in a very fair imitation of his man's expressionless voice:

'Mr West hasn't come in yet. What do you want with him at this time of night?'

'Hasn't come in yet, eh? Very well, then, I think we'd better come in and wait for him.'

'No, you don't.'

'See here, my man, my name is Inspector Verall of Scotland Yard, and I've got a warrant for the arrest of your master. You can see it if you like.'

Dermot perused the proffered paper, or pretended to do so, asking in a dazed voice:

'What for? What's he done?'

'Murder. Sir Alington West of Harley Street.'

His brain in a whirl, Dermot fell back before his redoubtable visitors. He went into the sitting-room and switched on the light. The inspector followed him.

'Have a search round,' he directed the other man. Then he turned to Dermot.

'You stay here, my man. No slipping off to warn your master. What's your name, by the way?'

'Milson, sir.'

'What time do you expect your master in, Milson?'

'I don't know, sir, he was going to a dance, I believe. At the Grafton Galleries.'

'He left there just under an hour ago. Sure he's not been back here?'

'I don't think so, sir. I fancy I should have heard him come in.'

At this moment the second man came in from the adjoining room. In his hand he carried the revolver. He took it across to the inspector in some excitement. An expression of satisfaction flitted across the latter's face.

'That settles it,' he remarked. 'Must have slipped in and out without your hearing him. He's hooked it by now. I'd better be off. Cawley, you stay here, in case he should come back again, and you keep an eye on this fellow. He may know more about his master than he pretends.'

The inspector bustled off. Dermot endeavoured to get at the details of the affair from Cawley, who was quite ready to be talkative.

'Pretty clear case,' he vouchsafed. 'The murder was discovered almost immediately. Johnson, the manservant, had only just gone up to bed when he fancied he heard a shot, and came down again. Found Sir Alington dead, shot through the heart. He rang us up at once and we came along and heard his story.'

'Which made it a pretty clear case?' ventured Dermot.

'Absolutely. This young West came in with his uncle and they were quarrelling when Johnson brought in the drinks. The old boy was threatening to make a new will, and your master was talking about shooting him. Not five minutes later the shot was heard. Oh! yes, clear enough. Silly young fool.'

Clear enough indeed. Dermot's heart sank as he realized the overwhelming nature of the evidence against him. Danger indeed—horrible danger! And no way out save that of flight. He set his wits to work. Presently he suggested making a cup of tea. Cawley assented readily enough. He had already searched the flat and knew there was no back entrance.

Dermot was permitted to depart to the kitchen. Once there he put the kettle on, and chinked cups and saucers industriously. Then he stole swiftly to the window and lifted the sash. The flat was on the second floor, and outside the window was a small wire lift used by tradesmen which ran up and down on its steel cable.

Like a flash Dermot was outside the window and swinging himself down the wire rope. It cut into his hands, making them bleed, but he went on desperately.

A few minutes later he was emerging cautiously from the back of the block. Turning the corner, he cannoned into a figure standing by the sidewalk. To his utter amazement he recognized Jack Trent. Trent was fully alive to the perils of the situation.

'My God! Dermot! Quick, don't hang about here.'

Taking him by the arm, he led him down a by-street, then down another. A lonely taxi was sighted and hailed and they jumped in, Trent giving the man his own address.

'Safest place for the moment. There we can decide what to do next to put those fools off the track. I came round here hoping to be able to warn you before the police got here, but I was too late.'

'I didn't even know that you had heard of it. Jack, you don't believe—'

'Of course not, old fellow, not for one minute. I know you far too well. All the same, it's a nasty business for you. They came round asking questions—what time you got to the Grafton Galleries, when you left, etc. Dermot, who could have done the old boy in?'

'I can't imagine. Whoever did it put the revolver in my drawer, I suppose. Must have been watching us pretty closely.'

'That séance business was damned funny. "Don't go home." Meant for poor old West. He did go home, and got shot.'

'It applies to me to,' said Dermot. 'I went home and found a planted revolver and a police inspector.'

'Well, I hope it doesn't get me too,' said Trent. 'Here we are.'

He paid the taxi, opened the door with his latch-key, and guided Dermot up the dark stairs to his den, which was a small room on the first floor.

He threw open the door and Dermot walked in, whilst Trent switched on the light, and then came to join him.

'Pretty safe here for the time being,' he remarked. 'Now we can get our heads together and decide what is best to be done.'

'I've made a fool of myself,' said Dermot suddenly. 'I ought to have faced it out. I see more clearly now. The whole thing's a plot. What the devil are you laughing at?'

For Trent was leaning back in his chair, shaking with unrestrained mirth. There was something horrible in the sound—something horrible, too, about the man altogether. There was a curious light in his eyes.

'A damned clever plot,' he gasped out. 'Dermot, my boy, you're done for.'

He drew the telephone towards him.

'What are you going to do?' asked Dermot.

'Ring up Scotland Yard. Tell 'em their bird's here—safe under lock and key. Yes, I locked the door when I came in and the key's in my pocket. No good looking at that other door behind me. That leads into Claire's room, and she always locks it on her side. She's afraid of me, you know. Been afraid of me a long time. She always knows when I'm thinking about that knife—a long sharp knife. No, you don't—'

Dermot had been about to make a rush at him, but the other had suddenly produced an ugly-looking revolver.

'That's the second of them,' chuckled Trent. 'I put the first of them in your drawer—after shooting old West with it—What are you looking at over my head? That door? It's no use, even if Claire was to open it—and she might to you—I'd shoot you before you got there. Not in the heart—not to kill, just wing you, so that you couldn't get away. I'm a jolly good shot, you know. I saved your life once. More fool I. No, no, I want you hanged—yes, hanged. It isn't you I want the knife for. It's Claire—pretty Claire, so white and soft. Old West knew. That's what he was here for tonight, to see if I was mad or not. He wanted to shut me up—so that I shouldn't get Claire with the knife. I was very cunning. I took his latchkey and yours too. I slipped away from the dance as soon as I got there. I saw you come out from his house, and

I went in. I shot him and came away at once. Then I went to your place and left the revolver. I was at the Grafton Galleries again almost as soon as you were, and I put the latch-key back in your coat pocket when I was saying good night to you. I don't mind telling you all this. There's no one else to hear, and when you're being hanged I'd like you to know I did it . . . There's not a loophole of escape. It makes me laugh . . . God, how it makes me laugh! What are you thinking of? What the devil are you looking at?'

'I'm thinking of some words you quoted just now. You'd have done better, Trent, not to come home.'

'What do you mean?'

'Look behind you!' Trent spun round. In the doorway of the communicating room stood Claire—and Inspector Verall . . .

Trent was quick. The revolver spoke just once—and found its mark. He fell forward across the table. The inspector sprang to his side, as Dermot stared at Claire in a dream. Thoughts flashed through his brain disjointedly. His uncle—their quarrel—the colossal misunderstanding—the divorce laws of England which would never free Claire from an insane husband—'we must all pity her'—the plot between her and Sir

Alington which the cunning of Trent had seen through—her cry to him, 'Ugly—ugly—ugly!' Yes, but now—

The inspector straightened up again.

'Dead,' he said vexedly.

'Yes,' Dermot heard himself saying, 'he was always a good shot . . .'

# Chapter 4

## The Chocolate Box

It was a wild night. Outside, the wind howled malevolently, and the rain beat against the windows in great gusts.

Poirot and I sat facing the hearth, our legs stretched out to the cheerful blaze. Between us was a small table. On my side of it stood some carefully brewed hot toddy; on Poirot's was a cup of thick, rich chocolate which I would not have drunk for a hundred pounds! Poirot sipped the thick brown mess in the

pink china cup, and sighed with content-
ment.

'Quelle belle vie!' he murmured.

'Yes, it's a good old world,' I agreed. 'Here
am I with a job, and a good job too! And
here are you, famous—'

'Oh, mon ami!' protested Poirot.

'But you are. And rightly so! When I think
back on your long line of successes, I
am positively amazed. I don't believe you
know what failure is!'

'He would be a droll kind of original who
could say that!'

'No, but seriously, have you ever failed?'

'Innumerable times, my friend. What
would you? La bonne chance, it cannot
always be on your side. I have been

called in too late. Very often another, working towards the same goal, has arrived there first. Twice have I been stricken down with illness just as I was on the point of success. One must take the downs with the ups, my friend.'

'I didn't quite mean that,' I said. 'I meant, had you ever been completely down and out over a case through your own fault?'

'Ah, I comprehend! You ask if I have ever made the complete prize ass of myself, as you say over here? Once, my friend—' A slow, reflective smile hovered over his face. 'Yes, once I made a fool of myself.'

He sat up suddenly in his chair.

'See here, my friend, you have, I know, kept a record of my little successes. You shall add one more story to the collection, the story of a failure!'

He leaned forward and placed a log on the fire. Then, after carefully wiping his hands on a little duster that hung on a nail by the fireplace, he leaned back and commenced his story.

That of which I tell you (said M. Poirot) took place in Belgium many years ago. It was at the time of the terrible struggle in France between church and state. M. Paul Déroulard was a

French deputy of note. It was an open secret that the portfolio of a Minister awaited him.

He was among the bitterest of the anti--Catholic party, and it was certain that on his accession to power, he would have to face violent enmity. He was in many ways a peculiar man. Though he neither drank nor smoked, he was nevertheless not so scrupulous in other ways. You comprehend, Hastings, c'était des femmes—toujours des femmes!

He had married some years earlier a young lady from Brussels who had brought him a substantial dot. Undoubtedly the money was useful to him in his career, as his family was not rich, though on the other hand he was entitled to call himself M. le Baron if he chose. There were no children of the marriage, and his wife died after two years—the result of a fall downstairs. Among the property which she bequeathed to him was a house on the Avenue Louise in Brussels.

It was in this house that his sudden death took place, the event coinciding with the resignation of the Minister whose portfolio he was to inherit. All the papers printed long notices of his career. His death, which had taken place quite suddenly in the evening after dinner, was attributed to heart-failure.

At that time, mon ami, I was, as you know, a member of the Belgian detective force. The death of M. Paul Déroulard was not particularly interesting to me. I am, as you also know, bon catholique, and his demise seemed to me fortunate.

It was some three days afterwards, when my vacation had just begun, that I received a visitor at my own apartments—a lady, heavily veiled, but evidently quite young; and I perceived at once that she was a jeune fille tout à fait comme il faut.

'You are Monsieur Hercule Poirot?' she asked in a low sweet voice.

I bowed.

'Of the detective service?'

Again I bowed. 'Be seated, I pray of you, mademoiselle,' I said.

She accepted a chair and drew aside her veil. Her face was charming, though marred with tears, and haunted as though with some poignant anxiety.

'Monsieur,' she said, 'I understand that you are now taking a vacation. Therefore you will be free to take up a private case.

You understand that I do not wish to call in the police.'

I shook my head. 'I fear what you ask is impossible, mademoiselle. Even though on vacation, I am still of the police.'

She leaned forward. 'Ecoutez, monsieur. All that I ask of you is to investigate. The result of your investigations you are at perfect liberty to report to the police. If what I believe to be true is true, we shall need all the machinery of the law.'

That placed a somewhat different complexion on the matter, and I placed myself at her service without more ado.

A slight colour rose in her cheeks. 'I thank you, monsieur. It is the death of M. Paul Déroulard that I ask you to investigate.'

'Comment?' I exclaimed, surprised.

'Monsieur, I have nothing to go upon—nothing but my woman's instinct, but I am convinced—convinced, I tell you—that M. Déroulard did not die a natural death!'

'But surely the doctors—'

'Doctors may be mistaken. He was so robust, so strong. Ah, Monsieur Poirot, I beseech of you to help me—'

The poor child was almost beside herself. She would have knelt to me. I soothed her as best I could.

'I will help you, mademoiselle. I feel almost sure that your fears are unfounded, but we will see. First, I will ask you to describe to me the inmates of the house.'

'There are the domestics, of course, Jeannette, Félice, and Denise the cook. She has been there many years; the others are simple country girls. Also there is François, but he too is an old servant. Then there is Monsieur Déroulard's mother who lived with him, and myself. My name is Virginie Mesnard. I am a poor cousin of the late Madame Déroulard, M. Paul's wife, and I have been a member of their ménage for over three years. I have now described to you the household. There were also two guests staying in the house.'

'And they were?'

'M. de Saint Alard, a neighbour of M. Déroulard's in France. Also an English friend, Mr John Wilson.'

'Are they still with you?'

'Mr Wilson, yes, but M. de Saint Alard departed yesterday.'

'And what is your plan, Mademoiselle Mesnard?'

'If you will present yourself at the house in half an hour's time, I will have arranged some story to account for your presence. I had better represent you to be connected with journalism in some way. I shall say you have come from Paris, and that you have brought a card of introduction from M. de Saint Alard. Madame Déroulard is very feeble in health, and will pay little attention to details.'

On mademoiselle's ingenious pretext I was admitted to the house, and after a brief interview with the dead deputy's mother, who was a wonderfully imposing and aristocratic figure though obviously in failing health, I was made free of the premises. I wonder, my friend (continued Poirot), whether you can possibly figure to yourself the difficulties of my task? Here was a man whose death had taken place three days previously. If there had been foul play, only one possibility was admittable—poison! And I had no chance of seeing the body, and there was no possibility of examining, or analysing, any medium in which the poison could have been administered. There were no clues, false or otherwise, to consider. Had the man been poisoned? Had he died a natural death? I, Hercule Poirot, with nothing to help me, had to decide.

First, I interviewed the domestics, and with their aid, I recapitulated the evening. I paid especial notice to the food at dinner, and the method of serving it. The soup had been served by M. Déroulard himself from a tureen. Next a dish of cutlets, then a chicken. Finally, a compote of fruits. And all placed on the table, and served by Monsieur himself. The coffee was brought in a big pot to the dinner-table. Nothing there, mon ami— impossible to poison one without poisoning all!

After dinner Madame Déroulard had retired to her own apartments and Mademoiselle

Virginie had accompanied her. The three men had adjourned to M. Déroulard's study. Here they had chatted amicably for some time, when suddenly, without any warning, the deputy had fallen heavily to the ground. M. de Saint Alard had rushed out and told François to fetch the doctor immediately. He said it was without doubt an apoplexy, explained the man. But when the doctor arrived, the patient was past help.

Mr John Wilson, to whom I was presented by Mademoiselle Virginie, was what was known in those days as a regular John Bull Englishman, middle-aged and burly. His account, delivered in very British French, was substantially the same.

'Déroulard went very red in the face, and down he fell.'

There was nothing further to be found out there. Next I went to the scene of the tragedy, the study, and was left alone there at my own request. So far there was nothing to support Mademoiselle Mesnard's theory. I could not but believe that it was a delusion on her part. Evidently she had entertained a romantic passion for the dead man which had not permitted her to take a normal view of the case. Nevertheless, I searched the study with meticulous care. It was just possible that a hypodermic needle might have been introduced into the dead man's chair in such a way as to allow of a fatal injection. The minute puncture it would cause was likely to remain unnoticed. But I could discover no sign to support the theory. I flung myself down in the chair with a gesture of despair.

'Enfin, I abandon it!' I said aloud. 'There is not a clue anywhere! Everything is perfectly normal.'

As I said the words, my eyes fell on a large box of chocolates standing on a table near by, and my heart gave a leap. It might not be a clue to M. Déroulard's death, but here at least was something that was not normal. I lifted the lid. The box was full, untouched; not a chocolate was missing—but that only made the peculiarity that had caught my eye more striking. For, see you, Hastings, while the box itself was pink, the lid was blue. Now, one often sees a blue ribbon on a pink box, and vice versa, but a box of one colour, and a lid of another—no, decidedly—ça ne se voit jamais!

chocolates standing on
a table

I did not as yet see that this little incident was of any use to me, yet I determined to investigate it as being out of the ordinary. I rang the bell for François, and asked him if his late master had been fond of sweets. A faint melancholy smile came to his lips.

'Passionately fond of them, monsieur. He would always have a box of chocolates in the house. He did not drink wine of any kind, you see.'

'Yet this box has not been touched?' I lifted the lid to show him.

'Pardon, monsieur, but that was a new box purchased on the day of his death, the other being nearly finished.'

'Then the other box was finished on the day of his death,' I said slowly.

'Yes, monsieur, I found it empty in the morning and threw it away.'

'Did M. Déroulard eat sweets at all hours of the day?'

'Usually after dinner, monsieur.'

I began to see light.

'François,' I said, 'you can be discreet?'

'If there is need, monsieur.'

'Bon! Know, then, that I am of the police. Can you find me that other box?'

'Without doubt, monsieur. It will be in the dustbin.'

He departed, and returned in a few minutes with a dust-covered object. It was the duplicate of the box I held, save for the fact that this time the box was blue and the lid was pink. I thanked François, recommended him once more to be discreet, and left the house in the Avenue Louise without more ado.

Next I called upon the doctor who had attended M. Déroulard. With him I had a difficult task. He entrenched himself prettily behind a wall of learned phraseology, but I fancied that he was not quite as sure about the case as he would like to be.

'There have been many curious occurrences of the kind,' he observed, when I had managed to disarm him somewhat. 'A sudden fit of anger, a violent emotion—after a heavy dinner, c'est entendu—then, with an access of rage, the blood flies to the head, and pst!—there you are!'

'But M. Déroulard had had no violent emotion.'

'No? I made sure that he had been having a stormy altercation with M. de Saint Alard.' 'Why should he?'

'C'est évident!' The doctor shrugged his shoulders. 'Was not M. de Saint Alard a Catholic of the most fanatical? Their friendship was being ruined by this question of church and state. Not a day passed without discussions. To M. de Saint Alard, Déroulard appeared almost as Antichrist.'

This was unexpected, and gave me food for thought.

'One more question, Doctor: would it be possible to introduce a fatal dose of poison into a chocolate?'

'It would be possible, I suppose,' said the doctor slowly. 'Pure prussic acid would meet the case if there were no chance of evaporation, and a tiny globule of anything might be swallowed unnoticed—but it does not seem a very likely supposition. A chocolate full of morphine or strychnine—' He made a wry face. 'You comprehend, M. Poirot—one bite would be enough! The unwary one would not stand upon ceremony.'

'Thank you, M. le Docteur.'

I withdrew. Next I made inquiries of the chemists, especially those in the neighbourhood of the Avenue Louise. It is good to be of the police. I got the information I wanted without any trouble. Only in one case could I hear of any poison having been supplied to the house in question. This was some eye drops of atropine sulphate for Madame Déroulard. Atropine is a potent poison, and for the moment I was elated, but the symptoms of atropine poisoning are closely allied to those of ptomaine, and bear no resemblance to those I was studying. Besides, the prescription was an old one. Madame Déroulard had suffered from cataracts in both eyes for many years.

I was turning away discouraged when the chemist's voice called me back.

'Un moment, M. Poirot. I remember, the girl who brought that prescription, she said something about having to go on to the English chemist. You might try there.'

I did. Once more enforcing my official status, I got the information I wanted. On the day before M. Déroulard's death they had made up a prescription for Mr John Wilson. Not that there was any making up about it. They were simply little tablets of trinitrine. I asked if I might see some. He showed me them, and my heart beat faster—for the tiny tablets were of chocolate.

'Is it a poison?' I asked.

'No, monsieur.'

'Can you describe to me its effect?'

'It lowers the blood-pressure. It is given for some forms of heart trouble—angina pectoris for instance. It relieves the arterial tension. In arteriosclerosis—'

I interrupted him. 'Ma foi! This rigmarole says nothing to me. Does it cause the face to flush?'

'Certainly it does.'

'And supposing I ate ten—twenty of your little tablets, what then?'

'I should not advise you to attempt it,' he replied drily.

'And yet you say it is not poison?'

'There are many things not called poison which can kill a man,' he replied as before.

I left the shop elated. At last, things had begun to march!

I now knew that John Wilson had the means for the crime—but what about the motive? He had come to Belgium on business, and had asked M. Déroulard, whom he knew slightly, to put him up. There was apparently no way in which Déroulard's death could benefit him. Moreover, I discovered by inquiries in England that he had suffered for some years from that painful form of heart disease known as angina. Therefore he had a genuine right to have those tablets in his possession. Nevertheless, I was convinced that someone had gone to the chocolate box, opening the full one first by mistake, and had abstracted the contents of the last chocolate, cramming in instead as many little trinitrine tablets as it would hold. The chocolates were large ones. Between twenty or thirty tablets, I felt sure, could have been inserted. But who had done this?

There were two guests in the house. John Wilson had the means. Saint Alard had the motive. Remember, he was a fanatic, and there is no fanatic like a religious fanatic. Could he, by any means, have got hold of John Wilson's trinitrine?

Another little idea came to me. Ah, you smile at my little ideas! Why had Wilson run out of trinitrine? Surely he would bring an adequate supply from England. I called once more at the house in the Avenue Louise. Wilson was out, but I saw the girl who did his room, Félice. I demanded of her immediately whether it was not true that M. Wilson had lost a bottle from his washstand some little time ago. The girl responded eagerly. It was quite true. She, Félice, had been blamed for it. The English gentleman had evidently thought that she had broken it, and did not like to say so. Whereas she had never even touched it. Without doubt it was Jeannette—always nosing round where she had no business to be—

I calmed the flow of words, and took my leave. I knew now all that I wanted to know. It remained for me to prove my case. That, I felt, would not be easy. I might be sure that Saint Alard had removed the bottle of trinitrine from John Wilson's washstand, but to convince others, I would have to produce evidence. And I had none to produce!

Never mind. I knew—that was the great thing. You remember our difficulty in the Styles case, Hastings? There again, I knew—but it took me a long time to find the last link which made my chain of evidence against the murderer complete.

I asked for an interview with Mademoiselle Mesnard. She came at once. I demanded of her the address of M. de Saint Alard. A look of trouble came over her face.

'Why do you want it, monsieur?'

'Mademoiselle, it is necessary.'

She seemed doubtful—troubled.

'He can tell you nothing. He is a man whose thoughts are not in this world. He hardly notices what goes on around him.'

'Possibly, mademoiselle. Nevertheless, he was an old friend of M. Déroulard's. There may be things he can tell me—things of the past—old grudges—old love-affairs.'

The girl flushed and bit her lip. 'As you please—but—but I feel sure now that I have been mistaken. It was good of you to accede to my demand, but I was upset—almost distraught at the time. I see now that there is no mystery to solve. Leave it, I beg of you, monsieur.'

I eyed her closely.

'Mademoiselle,' I said, 'it is sometimes difficult for a dog to find a scent, but once he has found it, nothing on earth will make him leave it! That is if he is a good dog! And I, mademoiselle, I, Hercule Poirot, am a very good dog.'

Without a word she turned away. A few minutes later she returned with the address written on a sheet of paper. I left the house. François was waiting for me outside. He looked at me anxiously.

'There is no news, monsieur?'

'None as yet, my friend.'

'Ah! Pauvre Monsieur Déroulard!' he sighed. 'I too was of his way of thinking. I do not care for priests. Not that I would say so in the house. The women are all devout—a good thing perhaps.

Madame est très pieuse—et Mademoi-selle Virginie aussi.'

Mademoiselle Virginie? Was she 'très pieuse?' Thinking of the tear-stained passionate face I had seen that first day, I wondered.

Having obtained the address of M. de Saint Alard, I wasted no time. I arrived in the neighbourhood of his château in the Ardennes but it was some days before I could find a pretext for gaining admission to the house. In the end I did—how do you think—as a plumber, mon ami! It was the affair of a moment to arrange a neat little gas leak in his bedroom. I departed for my tools, and took care to return with them at an hour when I knew I should have the field pretty well to myself. What I was searching for, I hardly knew. The one thing needful, I could not believe there was any chance of finding. He would never have run the risk of keeping it.

Still when I found the little cupboard above the washstand locked, I could not resist the temptation of seeing what was inside it. The lock was quite a simple one to pick. The door swung open. It was full of old bottles. I took them up one by one with a trembling hand. Suddenly, I uttered a cry. Figure to yourself, my friend, I held in my hand a little phial with an English chemist's label. On it were the words: 'Trinitrine Tablets. One to be taken when required. Mr John Wilson.'

I controlled my emotion, closed the cupboard, slipped the bottle into my pocket, and continued to repair the gas leak! One must be methodical. Then I left the château, and took train for my own country as soon as possible. I arrived in Brussels late that night. I was writing out a report for the préfet in the morning, when a note was brought to me. It was from old Madame Déroulard, and it summoned me to the house in the Avenue Louise without delay.

François opened the door to me.

'Madame la Baronne is awaiting you.'

He conducted me to her apartments. She sat in state in a large armchair. There was no sign of Mademoiselle Virginie.

'M. Poirot,' said the old lady, 'I have just learned that you are not what you pretend to be. You are a police officer.'

'That is so, madame.'

'You came here to inquire into the circumstances of my son's death?'

Again I replied: 'That is so, madame.'

'I should be glad if you would tell me what progress you have made.'

I hesitated.

'First I would like to know how you have learned all this, madame.'

'From one who is no longer of this world.'

Her words, and the brooding way she uttered them, sent a chill to my heart. I was incapable of speech.

'Therefore, monsieur, I would beg of you most urgently to tell me exactly what progress you have made in your investigation.'

'Madame, my investigation is finished.'

'My son?'

'Was killed deliberately.'

'You know by whom?'

'Yes, madame.'

'Who, then?'

'M. de Saint Alard.'

'You are wrong. M. de Saint Alard is incapable of such a crime.'

'The proofs are in my hands.'

'I beg of you once more to tell me all.'

This time I obeyed, going over each step that had led me to the discovery of the truth. She listened attentively. At the end she nodded her head.

'Yes, yes, it is all as you say, all but one thing. It was not M. de Saint Alard who killed my son. It was I, his mother.'

I stared at her. She continued to nod her head gently.

'It is well that I sent for you. It is the providence of the good God that Virginie told me before she departed for the convent, what she had done. Listen, M. Poirot! My son was an evil man. He persecuted the church. He led a life of mortal sin.

He dragged down the other souls beside his own. But there was worse than that. As I came out of my room in this house one morning, I saw my daughter-in-law standing at the head of the stairs. She was reading a letter. I saw my son steal up behind her. One swift push, and she fell, striking her head on the marble steps. When they picked her up she was dead. My son was a murderer, and only I, his mother, knew it.'

She closed her eyes for a moment. 'You cannot conceive, monsieur, of my agony, my despair. What was I to do? Denounce him to the police? I could not bring myself to do it. It was my duty, but my flesh was weak. Besides, would they believe me? My eyesight had been failing for some time—they would say I was mistaken. I kept silence. But my conscience gave me no peace. By keeping silence I too was a murderer. My son inherited his wife's money. He flourished as the green bay tree. And now he was to have a Minister's portfolio. His persecution of the church would be redoubled. And there was Virginie. She, poor child, beautiful, naturally pious, was fascinated by him. He had a strange and terrible power over women. I saw it coming. I was powerless to prevent it. He had no intention of marrying her. The time came when she was ready to yield everything to him.

'Then I saw my path clear. He was my son. I had given him life. I was responsible for him. He had killed one woman's body, now he would kill another's soul!

I went to Mr Wilson's room, and took the bottle of tablets. He had once said laughingly that there were enough in it to kill a man! I went into the study and opened the big box of chocolates that always stood on the table. I opened a new box by mistake. The other was on the table also. There was just one chocolate left in it. That simplified things. No one ate chocolates except my son and Virginie. I would keep her with me that night. All went as I had planned—'

She paused, closing her eyes a minute then opened them again.

'M. Poirot, I am in your hands. They tell me I have not many days to live. I am willing to answer for my action before the good God. Must I answer for it on earth also?'

I hesitated. 'But the empty bottle, madame,' I said to gain time. 'How came that into M. de Saint Alard's possession?'

'When he came to say goodbye to me, monsieur, I slipped it into his pocket. I did not know how to get rid of it. I am so infirm that I cannot move about much without help, and finding it empty in my rooms might have caused suspicion. You understand, monsieur—' she drew herself up to her full height—'it was with no idea of casting suspicion on M. de Saint Alard! I never dreamed of such a thing. I thought his valet would find an empty bottle and throw it away without question.'

I bowed my head. 'I comprehend, madame,' I said.

'And your decision, monsieur?'

Her voice was firm and unfaltering, her head held as high as ever.

I rose to my feet.

'Madame,' I said, 'I have the honour to wish you good day. I have made my investigations—and failed! The matter is closed.'

He was silent for a moment, then said quietly: 'She died just a week later. Mademoiselle Virginie passed through her novitiate, and duly took the veil. That, my friend, is the story. I must admit that I do not make a fine figure in it.'

'But that was hardly a failure,' I expostulated. 'What else could you have thought under the circumstances?'

'Ah, sacré, mon ami,' cried Poirot, becoming suddenly animated. 'Is it that you do not see?

But I was thirty-six times an idiot! My grey cells, they functioned not at all. The whole time I had the clue in my hands.'

'What clue?'

'The chocolate box! Do you not see? Would anyone in possession of their full eyesight make such a mistake? I knew Madame Déroulard had cataracts—the atropine drops told me that. There was only one person in the household whose eyesight was such that she could not see which lid to replace. It was the chocolate box that started me on the track, and yet up to the end I failed consistently to perceive its real significance!

'Also my psychology was at fault. Had M. de Saint Alard been the criminal, he would never have kept an incriminating bottle. Finding it was a proof of his innocence. I had learned already from Mademoiselle Virginie that he was absent--minded. Altogether it was a miserable affair that I have recounted to you there! Only to you have I told the story. You comprehend, I do not figure well in it! An old lady commits a crime in such a simple and clever fashion that I, Hercule Poirot, am completely deceived. Sapristi! It does not bear thinking of! Forget it. Or no—remember it, and if you think at any time that I am growing conceited—it is not likely, but it might arise.'

I concealed a smile.

'Eh bien, my friend, you shall say to me, "Chocolate box". Is it agreed?'

'It's a bargain!'

'After all,' said Poirot reflectively, 'it was an experience! I, who have undoubtedly the finest brain in Europe at present, can afford to be magnanimous!'

'Chocolate box,' I murmured gently.

'Pardon, mon ami?'

I looked at Poirot's innocent face, as he bent forward inquiringly, and my heart smote me.

I had suffered often at his hands, but I, too, though not possessing the finest brain in Europe, could afford to be mag-nanimous!

'Nothing,' I lied, and lit another pipe, smiling to myself.

# Hey book lovers and adventurers...

H ey book lovers and adventure seekers, time to dive into the thrilling world of classic books at our website and discover endless excitement!

https://lambda-press.my.canva.site/

Printed in Great Britain
by Amazon

40412840R00128